A Song for Cecilia Fantini

by
Cynthia Astor

illustrated by
Anthony Turpin

H J Kramer
Starseed Press
Tiburon, CA

For Desiree, beloved granddaughter.
May the light of your mother's memory
remain bright within you.
C. A.

To Russell Frost, friend, mentor,
an artist's artist.
T. T.

H J Kramer Inc
P.O. Box 1082
Tiburon, CA 94920

Library of Congress Cataloging-in-Publication Data
Astor, Cynthia.
  A song for Cecilia Fantini / by Cynthia Astor ; illustrated by
Anthony Turpin.
     p.   cm.
  Summary: When her beloved music teacher dies suddenly,
Emmaline tries to find indelible ways to remember her always.
  ISBN 0-915811-75-8
  [1. Death—Fiction. 2. Grief—Fiction. 3. Music—Fiction.]
I. Turpin, Anthony, ill. II. Title.
PZ7.A8485So   1997   96–37539
[Fic]—dc21   CIP
                                                    AC
Printed in Singapore.
10 9 8 7 6 5 4 3 2 1

Emmaline fairly flew down the stairs, pulling on her coat as she went. It was Tuesday, the day she went for her music lesson with Cecilia Fantini. Mrs. Fantini had been the music teacher at the elementary school on Willoughby Island for forty years. When she retired, she began teaching students at her home. Emmaline's mother had learned to play the piano from her when she was a child, and everyone on Willoughby Island who loved music had learned to love it with Cecilia Fantini.

Emmaline had been studying piano and voice for four years. She sang in the children's choir at church and in the school chorus. She sang at recitals and in Christmas pageants. She even sang at a wedding once. At the age of ten, she was an accomplished musician and Mrs. Fantini's star pupil.

Despite the hard work, Emmaline loved her lessons with Mrs. Fantini. The cozy room welcomed her with its grand piano and the stacks of music everywhere, all musty smelling and dusty. Most of all, she loved the last part of her lesson, when Mrs. Fantini would play the piano and the two of them would sing duets.

"Music resides in a special place, somewhere between your head and your heart. Somewhere between math and magic," Mrs. Fantini would say. "Once inside you, it is a part of you forever and never disappears."

"Now, we make music together. Emmaline, you will sing like a nightingale," Mrs. Fantini said, as she played the first notes of their favorite song. It was an old Welsh air, and they ended each lesson with it. Mrs. Fantini had taught this song to every one of her music students:

Sleep, my love, and peace attend thee,
All through the night.
Guardian angels God will send thee,
All through the night.

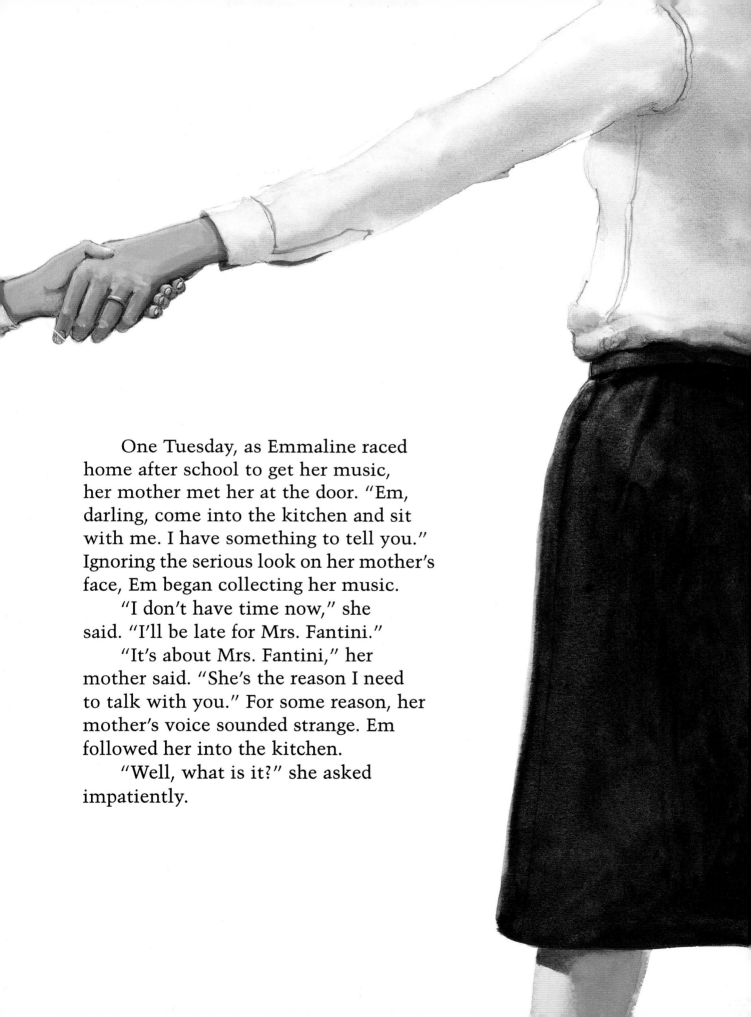

One Tuesday, as Emmaline raced
home after school to get her music,
her mother met her at the door. "Em,
darling, come into the kitchen and sit
with me. I have something to tell you."
Ignoring the serious look on her mother's
face, Em began collecting her music.

"I don't have time now," she
said. "I'll be late for Mrs. Fantini."

"It's about Mrs. Fantini," her
mother said. "She's the reason I need
to talk with you." For some reason, her
mother's voice sounded strange. Em
followed her into the kitchen.

"Well, what is it?" she asked
impatiently.

"You know, Em," her mother said as they both sat down, "Mrs. Fantini is quite old, almost eighty, I think. When you live that long, things can happen to your body. Some parts may not work very well, and some parts may stop working entirely. Mrs. Fantini had a heart attack this morning, Em, and she died before anyone could get her to the hospital."

Emmaline stared blankly at her mother. She had a funny, twisting feeling deep inside her. Tears were streaming down her mother's face now, and this frightened Emmaline.

"You mean she died forever?" she asked, knowing within that this was so, that dear Mrs. Fantini was gone forever. She thought of the duets they had sung together last week, how gay and spirited the songs had been. Slowly, warm tears rolled down her cheeks and fell silently onto her music.

Today was Friday, the day that Emmaline would say her final good-bye to Mrs. Fantini. It was the first time she had ever been to a funeral, and she was very nervous about what to expect. Her mother told her that everyone who knew and loved Cecilia Fantini would come to say their good-byes. She said that Mrs. Fantini's body would be in a casket at the front of the chapel, and that prayers would be said, songs would be sung, and words would be spoken about her life. Still, Em was not prepared for the many people who gathered. It looked as if everyone on the whole island was there. As she sat holding her mother's hand, her mother turned to her and said, "Just look, Em, all these people came to honor Mrs. Fantini and express their love for her. All these people."

They all looked very sad to Emmaline. Some sobbed, and others talked quietly to one another. Some sat with their heads bowed. Though she didn't cry, Em felt very sad, too. She knew she would never see Mrs. Fantini again. At the end of the service, as she passed by the casket, she whispered quietly, "Good-bye, Mrs. Fantini. I shall never forget you."

Time went by. It had been three months since Mrs. Fantini died. A strange thing was happening to Emmaline. She couldn't quite see Mrs. Fantini's face anymore, and she couldn't quite hear her voice. She had a photograph of herself and Mrs. Fantini playing at a recital. It sat on her dresser, and every day she studied it intently. The picture in its frame remained clear, but somehow, inside of Em, Mrs. Fantini was beginning to fade. This bothered Em greatly, and made her feel disloyal in a way she couldn't understand. She had promised she would never forget, so why was this happening? Emmaline refused to take lessons from Augustus McQuin, the music teacher at the elementary school. In fact, she hadn't even felt like playing the piano or singing at all in the last three months. When she was feeling particularly sad, she'd think about the duets, and she'd hear the music clearly, inside, just as Mrs. Fantini had promised.

One day, Emmaline decided that there must be ways for her to remember Mrs. Fantini. Not everyone who had known her would forget so quickly, Em was sure.

She decided she would ask Morris Kaminski, who owned the Island Deli. He was almost as old as Mrs. Fantini and had known her all of his life. Emmaline entered the deli.

"Well, hello, Em," he said, smiling. "Come for some more pickles, have you?"

"Not really," Em said quietly. "I've come to ask you a question." She couldn't tell him that her memory of Mrs. Fantini was fading, so she simply asked, "How do you remember Mrs. Fantini?"

Mr. Kaminski looked at Emmaline intently.

"Music, of course," said Mr. Kaminski. "Certain pieces of music that she used to sing will always remind me of Cecilia Fantini. Remember how she closed each of her recitals with her special song?" With tears in his eyes, he sang a few notes softly:

> *Soft the drowsy hours are creeping,*
> *Hill and dale in slumber sleeping.*
> *Love alone his watch is keeping,*
> *All through the night.*

"That's the same song we'd sing at the end of the lesson," Em said.

"I know," replied Mr. Kaminski. "It was her favorite."

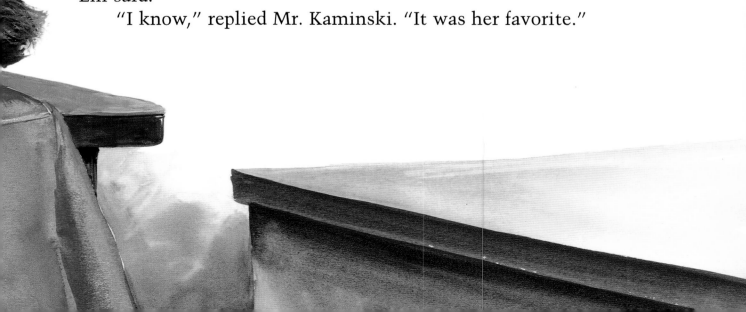

"In the Jewish tradition, we place a stone on the grave when we go to visit," he continued. "I always take a pebble that I find along the beach to leave at her grave. Come, you and I, we will find that one special stone with which to remember Cecilia Fantini."

The morning was warm and the wind was calm as they searched among the rocks and shells. Emmaline found a perfect sand dollar shell with its delicate leaf design, and Morris Kaminski chose a blue stone as smooth as glass.

"Now, we can go to visit," said Mr. Kaminski, "and we will place these upon her gravestone. This is our way of promising that she will never be forgotten."

The next day, Emmaline decided to visit the Village Bookstore owned by Isabella Starling. All the children on Willoughby Island knew her as Star, and they all flocked into her store every Saturday morning for her storytelling hour. She would dress up in a costume to match the story, and she would use different voices for each character. Sometimes, when it was a very special tale, Cecilia Fantini had played the piano.

"How do you remember Mrs. Fantini?" Em asked Star after they had settled comfortably among the many pillows in the story room.

"I write to her on the wings of a butterfly," Star said with a smile as she unfolded a beautiful kite in the shape of a butterfly. "I send her a letter. I tell her how much I miss her, and I tell her about things that have happened since she died. Then, I decide on a special place to go to remember her. Sometimes, I go up to the top of Wildcat Hill. Sometimes, I go to the cove by Ten Mile Point. Wherever I am, I fly the butterfly as high as I can to send the message into the clouds. As the kite circles and dives, I sing a few lines from her favorite song to guide it on its way."

"May I write her a letter now?" Emmaline asked excitedly.

"Of course," Star said, handing Emmaline the kite. "I'll go find some string, and when you're ready, we'll go to any spot you pick."

As they arrived at the top of South
Bluff, at the very tip of Willoughby Island,
the wind was blowing strongly from the
west. "Let's sing a little of her song," Star
said. As the kite rose in the sky, she and
Emmaline sang:

> *Hark! A solemn bell is ringing,*
> *Clear through the night.*
> *Thou, my love, are heavenward*
>   *winging,*
> *Home through the night.*

Emmaline knew there was at least one other person she had to visit. She hadn't wanted to go back to the house before, but now she was anxious to get there. She was sure that Mr. Fantini, of all people, would know of a special way to remember his wife.

As Mr. Fantini ushered her into the music room, Em felt both sad and comforted.

"How do you remember her?" Emmaline asked.

"Her music and her spirit fill this house. On all important days, like her birthday, holidays, the day we were married, and the day she died, I light a candle in her memory and let it burn all day. The light from that candle lights this house, just as she did."

Quietly, Mr. Fantini began to sing the words of her song:

Earthly dust from off thee shaken,
All immortal thou shall waken.
Peace, my love, in journey taken,
Home through the night.

When the song was ended, they sat in silence for a while. Then Mr. Fantini turned to Emmaline and said, "She would want you to continue with your music, Emmaline. It's time to begin again."

The following day, Em woke up with the feeling that it might be okay to talk to her mother about music lessons with Mr. McQuin.

"Mrs. Fantini would want me to," she told her mother, as they worked together planting the spring flowers. "Remember how she used to say I should sing like a nightingale? Well, I won't be able to unless I keep practicing."

Augustus McQuin was waiting for Emmaline at four o'clock that very afternoon.

"Before we begin our lessons, Emmaline, I wonder if you would come with me to sing a song for Mrs. Fantini."

"I'd like that," said Em, knowing exactly what he had in mind.

As they walked together across town, Em told him about the shell and the stone that she and Morris Kaminski left on the gravestone, and about the butterfly kite that she and Star sent soaring into the clouds, and about the candle that she lit with Mr. Fantini.

As they stood together near her grave, Emmaline knew that, like music, Mrs. Fantini's memory would be a part of her forever.

"Now, we make music together," Mr. McQuin said. Softly, they began to sing a song, a song for Cecilia Fantini.